I May Fly

By Brandon Baxter

Illustrated by Shannon Lloyd

I May Fly © 2019 by Brandon Baxter

All rights reserved. No part of this book may be reproduced, distributed or transmitted in any form or by any means, without written permission from the publisher, except in the noncommercial uses permitted by copyright law. For permission requests, contact Permissions Coordinator, sealofterspress@gmail.com

Oh, hey! My name is May.

I'm May Fly.

I'm a fly.

I'm a mayfly.

Someday, I may fly.

I may fly far, far away.

I may fly tomorrow or today.

I may fly around the world.

I may fly like a baseball, hurled.

I may fly across the street.

Or perhaps I'll walk,

just use my feet.

Some believe I won't fly at all.

Perhaps it's because

they think I'm too small.

I will get bigger, this I know.

My little wings will continue to grow.

When I'm ready and whatever will be…

That's when my wings will carry me!

I'm May Fly and I WILL fly.

You'll see!

The End

About the Author

Brandon Baxter is a father, writer, listener and conversationalist. Spending his early years as a sports producer for local news in Cleveland, Ohio, Brandon honed his writing technique while creating nightly content for sports anchors and reporters. Brandon's story telling has always come naturally, presenting it in print has become his outlet for creativity and expression.

About the Illustrator

Shannon Lloyd is a part-time children's book illustrator and a full-time college student, hailing from Strongsville, Ohio. Pursuing her B.F.A. in Animation at the University of Louisiana at Lafayette, Shannon's creativity and drive for excellence has assisted in developing her digital illustration skills through perseverance and the loving support of her friends and family.

44033775R00015

Made in the USA
Middletown, DE
02 May 2019